SNAKE
in My Toilet

A novel by

G.T. Sherman

HIP-JR.

HIP Junior

Library and Archives Canada Cataloguing in Publication

Sherman, Gisela Tobien, 1947-, author
   Snake in my toilet / Gisela Sherman.

(HIP jr)

ISBN 978-1-926847-48-1

   I. Title. II. Series: HIP jr

PS8587.H3857S63 2014   jC813'.54   C2013-908665-X

General editor: Paul Kropp
Text design and typesetting: Laura Brady
Illustrator: Charlie Hnatiuk
Cover design: Robert Corrigan

1 2 3 4 5 6 7   20 19 18 17 16 15 14

Printed in Canada

High Interest Publishing acknowledges the financial support of
the Government of Canada through the Canada Book Fund for
our publishing activities.

There's a giant snake loose in the apartment building. He keeps showing up in the most embarrassing places. Can Cam find the snake before he gets hurt ... or killed?

CHAPTER 1

Two Snakes

I did not want to go outside at the lunch break. DK was outside, in the schoolyard, and he was waiting for me. DK has big arms for punching kids like me. DK has a big mouth for cursing kids like me. DK is a problem for kids like me.

So I thought I'd be safe in the washroom. And I was ... until Mr. Hogan saw me.

"Cameron," he yelled at me. "Get outside."

"I can't," I replied.

"Why not?" Mr. Hogan asked. Mr. Hogan eats

Kindergarten kids for breakfast. Mr. Hogan is afraid of nothing. No way I could tell him that I was scared of DK.

So I shrugged.

Mr. Hogan glared at me. His upper lip curled up. It looked like his moustache grew out of his nose. "Grade 8 kids need to run. You guys need to build muscles. So get out in the schoolyard, Cam. Like, now!"

What choice did I have?

I walked outside as slowly as I dared. I looked around. Next to the school, I saw a circle of kids. That should be good, I thought. Safety in numbers.

But as I got closer, I saw DK in the middle of the circle. He was swinging something back and forth. He kept moving closer and closer toward Jade Paz, a grade 7 girl. Jade is the kind of girl who wears a new color of nail polish each day. The kind who picks a cell phone to match her shoes. But today Jade looked scared.

Jade was staring at what DK had in his hand. And she didn't like it.

The school wall blocked her from moving back. Kids stood all around her. Jade was cornered.

I watched, just like the other guys. What was it? What was DK doing?

A snake! DK was swinging a garter snake in Jade's face. Talk about gross!

Poor Jade looked around for help. I wanted to do something. I bet the other guys did too. But no one moved. No one wanted to be DK's next victim.

DK laughed. He threw the snake right at Jade. It hit her face, then dropped to the shoulder of her frilly pink top.

But Jade was cool. She looked at DK as if he were toe jam. She reached to her shoulder and pulled off the snake. She dropped it daintily into some bushes and the snake slid out of sight.

"Slime," she said. Maybe she was talking about the snake, maybe about DK. Then, holding her head high, Jade walked away.

I wanted to clap for her, but I was nervous about DK. A girl had made a fool of him. Now he'd be looking for another victim.

That's when DK saw me. "Whatcha smiling at, Cameron?" he snarled. "You want to be next?"

* * *

That night I dreamed of giant snakes. They had teeth the size of scissors. They chased me, but I couldn't run. I was doomed to become snake snack – at least in my dream.

When I woke up, my room was as dark as a cave. I checked the time. Three o'clock. The zeros on the digital clock looked like two snake eyes.

Half-asleep, I walked to the bathroom. Two yellow eyes glared at me from the toilet. I blinked and looked again. Something dark filled the toilet bowl. Something *moved* in the toilet bowl.

It looked like a snake. A snake?

"A snake!" I screamed. "A snake! A snake in the toilet!"

Footsteps pounded down the hall. My mom and my older sister rushed in. One of them turned on the light.

I stood frozen to the spot, still screaming. My mom grabbed me and checked for blood. "What's wrong, Cameron?"

"A snake!" I hissed. "There's a snake in the toilet."

"Eeuw!" screeched my sister, Ella. She hates anything that's creepy or crawly. Sometimes I think she's not that crazy about me, either.

We all looked down at the toilet bowl. It was empty.

Ella rolled her eyes. Mom wasn't thrilled either. She led me back to my bedroom like I was a baby. Then she sat and rubbed my back. "You just had a nightmare, Cam."

"Yeah, maybe, but . . ."

"It was just a bad dream," she repeated. It was her soothing voice. It was her I-don't-believe-a-thing-you-said voice.

By the time she left, I kind of thought she was right. After all, who ever heard of a snake in the toilet?

CHAPTER 2

Caterpillar Guts

Tuesday morning I woke up early. I badly needed to pee. Was the snake a bad dream? I sure hoped so. I tiptoed across the hall and peeked into the bathroom. Nothing.

Dummy, I said to myself. What did you expect? A cobra brushing his fangs?

I made myself march to the toilet. Then I stood there, glad to be a boy. I could do my job standing up with my eyes on the toilet bowl. There would be no surprises down there.

No snakes. No surprises. I must have dreamed the whole thing.

I had time to play a computer game before school. It was fun to be a hero for a change. I felt so good I put on the special T-shirt my dad gave me. Now he's back in Panama, working on the new canal. I won't see him for months, Mom says.

Still, I walked to school with a smile on my face. It was the kind of sunny May morning that made me feel good. Maybe DK was away today. Maybe my dad would let me visit him in Panama. Maybe some girl like Jade would notice me.

At school, I did okay in my math test. DK wasn't around at recess. Life was good.

Until lunch time.

After we eat at my school, we have to go outside. We hang out in the playground. Some kids have friends. Some kids play sports. I watch kids swing from the climbers.

"Watch out!" someone said.

I jumped back. And I bumped into somebody. My bad luck – I bumped into DK.

"You jerk! Look what you did!" DK screamed.

"I, uh . . . sorry."

"My dessert!" DK went on "You made me drop my cupcake!"

I looked at DK's angry face. I stared at the smooshed cupcake on the ground. There was gravel stuck to the white icing. I looked up again, and DK was making fists with both hands.

Lucky for me, some teachers stood nearby. DK had to stay cool. Or cool enough. He gave me the finger and stomped away.

For the rest of the lunch hour I stood near the teachers. What else could I do?

But I knew that DK never forgets.

When the lunch bell rang, I felt okay. I had made it through lunch. DK was over with his buddies, by the running track.

Or so I thought.

Kids and teachers crowded to the doors. We lined up, and then someone shoved me from behind.

DK, I thought. It had to be DK.

DK pushed me again. Some guys stood and watched us. The teachers were . . . where?

I turned and saw DK grinning at me like a devil.

"Cameron, old buddy," DK said. "You didn't get my snake yesterday. But I have something else for you today."

He stepped closer and stuck out his hand.

I jumped back. Then I relaxed.

DK only held a caterpillar in his hand. A little brown caterpillar curled up in a fuzzy ball.

More guys saw the two of us. They figured there was a fight about to happen, so they came over to watch us. They wanted some action.

But I was okay. DK's little caterpillar didn't scare me. I laughed. "Gee thanks, DK. I love caterpillars."

I smiled. DK scowled.

Then I added one more thing. "Watch out he doesn't do number two on your hand."

Everybody laughed. I had scored!

But DK went crazy. In a flash, he dropped the caterpillar inside my T-shirt.

"You like him. He's yours!"

The caterpillar tickled as it crawled across my chest. I didn't like it, but I kept up the show. "Thanks. I'll keep it for a pet. I'll call it Dilmer."

That was DK's real name. And he hates it. Who can blame him?

That's when DK lost it. He came charging at

me like a crazy bull. His head slammed into my chest.

The pain burned red hot for a second, then I fell onto the ground. DK sat on top of me, pounding me with both fists.

By the time a teacher pulled him off, it was too late. DK had squashed the caterpillar on my chest. Green and yellow mush stained the front of my T-shirt.

My special T-shirt. The one from my dad.

I lay in the gravel and thought of my dad. Tears slid down my cheeks. I wiped them away, but it was too late. Kids were laughing at me.

I stood and brushed the dirt off myself. My big moment had come – and I'd blown it.

My nose was bleeding. A teacher handed me a tissue to clean the blood off my face.

She looked sorry for me. "Go wash yourself off, Cameron." She tried to quiet the other kids, but they got even louder.

"Crybaby! Crybaby! Crybaby!"

It felt like the whole world was chanting. I

could even hear them through the washroom windows as I cleaned my face.

Then I heard a voice behind me. "You're going to have one cool black eye."

"Yeah."

It was Jade's brother, Rafe. He's in the other grade 8 class. Rafe grinned at me through shiny braces.

"DK's a jerk," he said. "Don't let him spoil your day."

Easy for you to say, I thought. But it was good advice.

CHAPTER 3

Balls

It was a bad afternoon. Too many kids had seen me cry. Too many kids made jokes about my T-shirt. I wished it was time to go home. But last period, we had gym.

Mr. Hogan knew what had happened. So he treated me worse than ever. "Cameron! Boys your age lift their knees off the floor when they do push-ups. Got that?"

"Yes, sir."

"So give me twenty more!"

Mr. Hogan – the Hulk we always said behind his back – told us to play dodge ball. Great. I love being a target. I love having kids throw balls at my face.

It was okay for maybe ten minutes. Then, when Mr. Hogan wasn't looking, DK slammed the ball at me. He hit me – right where it really hurts.

I scrunched over in pain. My eyes stung. Tears began to fall from my eyes, no matter how hard I tried to stop them.

Mr. Hogan saw me crying. "What's wrong?" he barked.

"I don't know, sir. I think the ball hit Cam's knee," said DK.

Hogan's moustache went up his nose again. "For Pete's sake, boy, toughen up. And don't turn on the waterworks again."

The waterworks had already started. And the pain was like a hammer in my shorts. Kids were watching me. It was so unfair. I had to do something.

I grabbed the ball at my feet.

"Let's see how YOU like it, muscle-head!" I yelled. Then I threw the ball towards DK as hard as I could. It was a pretty strong throw. But in the wrong direction.

The ball hit Mr. Hogan – right where it had hit me!

The other kids were as surprised as I was.

What to do? I had a moment of pure panic, a

moment when all the blood raced to my brain. Then I ran out of the gym. Out of the school. All the way home.

I let myself into our apartment and flopped onto the couch. My heart pounded so hard I thought it would bust out of my chest. When I finally calmed down, the phone rang. I looked at the call display. My school was calling.

I didn't answer, but I knew they'd call my mom at work.

I was in huge trouble. Could my life get any worse?

I grabbed a Pepsi from the kitchen. Then, of course, I had to go pee. I opened the bathroom door and stepped inside.

I burped. No big deal.

But something burped back at me.

Down there, in the toilet bowl, was a huge snake. It was sliding out of the toilet bowl and onto the floor . . . and heading right toward me.

CHAPTER 4

Snake!

I turned and raced out of the apartment and into the hallway. I was wailing like a fire engine.

Two old guys were waiting by the stairs. They were Mr. Bell and Mr. Kim, the mean old guys who said I made too much noise.

And I was. "A snake!" I yelled at them.

"Where?" they asked together.

"In my toilet!"

"You kids and your dumb jokes," Mr. Bell said. "When are you going to grow up, Cameron?" He went to his apartment and slammed the door.

Mr. Kim just shrugged. He followed me to the bathroom.

"A snake?" he asked.

I pointed. Only the snake's head stuck out of the toilet now. Its tongue flicked out and in.

Mr. Kim groaned and slid to the floor. He lay there dead still and pale as paper.

I ran out to the hallway one more time. "Help!" I shouted.

A few people came outside.

"Mr. Kim fainted," I told them.

This time, six people followed me to my bathroom. Of course, the snake was gone.

One lady, a nurse, helped Mr. Kim sit up. The old guy was chalk white. "Get me out of here," he moaned. "I'm not staying near that snake."

The others looked around the bathroom. "Let's take this man to the living room for air," said the nurse. The eight of us rushed out so fast we got jammed in the doorway.

Someone must have called downstairs. In a

minute or two, Zoom Zess showed up at the door. Zoom is the super for our building. His name tells you just how fast he is.

"Now, what's going on here?" Zoom asked.

All of us told him, all at the same time. Then we were drowned out by sirens outside.

Soon two police officers walked in. "What's the problem?" one of them asked.

The nine of us told them all at once. More sirens drowned us out. An ambulance squealed to a halt at the front door. Two men carrying a stretcher rushed in.

By now the hall was full of staring people. They were like flies at a barbecue.

The ambulance guys rushed in. Other people came after them. Then someone knocked over a plant. Broken bits of clay and earth flew across the rug. Someone else stepped on it.

Our new rug. My mom would have a fit.

D'oh. My mom! She'd go crazy.

"Get out, everyone! Everything's okay. Go home!" I yelled. I pushed people to the door.

Then I heard the scream in the lobby. It was my mother.

When Mom got to our door, her hair was flying. Her eyes shone glassy and huge. "Cameron!" she screeched. "What's going on here?"

* * *

Mom cooled down when she saw I was safe. She gave the police a statement, and phoned the SPCA. She told all the people to leave us alone. By the time my sister came home, we were alone.

We told Ella about the snake in our toilet.

"A snake?" Ella asked.

"A snake," I said. Mom nodded

"A big snake?"

"Yeah, pretty big."

"A big slimy snake is in our bathroom?"

"Yup," I said.

My sister freaked out. She was still freaking when we heard a knock at the door. It was a man from the SPCA. That's our local animal shelter.

"I'm Officer Pat Piper," he said. "But please call me Pat." The man had curly brown hair, a long nose and droopy brown eyes. He looked like a hound dog left at the pound too long.

Pat asked me to tell him what happened. Then he poked around our bathroom. I wondered if he would sniff the toilet. But no.

"Anyone else see this snake?" he asked.

"Mr. Kim, down the hall," I said.

So we all walked two doors down. Then Mr. Kim told Pat what he saw. "I think it was a boa constrictor. It was a pale brown color but with dark brown triangles."

"I bet it was twice this long," I added. Then I stretched out my arms as wide as I could.

"No way," replied Pat. "Boas are the smallest of the big snakes. They grow only about two or three metres long. That's only six feet or so."

"Only!" my sister gasped. She turned to our mom and whined. "How am I supposed to use the bathroom? A snake is so gross."

"I'm sure we can use the Watts's bathroom

across the hall," Mom said. She's good in a crisis. Then she turned to Pat. "How soon can you catch that snake?"

Pat scratched his head. "Who knows? All the noise scared him away for now."

Mom turned pale. "For now?"

I was nervous. "What can you do?"

Pat stopped to think. "Well, we don't get a lot of these. I'll check with the office, but we can start with pouring hot water down your toilet. Snakes like to be warm. When this boa comes back to get warm, I'll grab him."

"You'll grab him?" I repeated.

Pat nodded. I guess that was no problem at all for him.

So we started pouring enough hot water to fill a swimming pool. Then we waited. It felt like watching a bad horror movie.

I was afraid to look at the toilet but I couldn't help sneaking peeks. Peeks at nothing.

At six o'clock Pat looked at his watch. "Okay, folks, I'm afraid that my shift is over. I'll come

back in the morning to see how you're doing."

"What! You can't leave now," said Mom. "You didn't catch the snake!"

"I'm going home for supper."

"Supper!" Mom got mad. "There's a killer snake in our toilet, and you're going home to eat?"

"Yup. Got some kids waiting for me. You'll be fine. Boas aren't dangerous."

"Not dangerous?" Mom screamed. "Not dangerous? They choke people to death!"

But Pat had already walked out of our apartment.

Mom, Ella and I looked at each other. We shut the bathroom door and got our own supper. We tried to forget about the snake.

Before we even started our soup, the first visitor knocked at our door. "Is the snake gone?" a lady from down the hall asked. She looked around as if there was a snake lurking behind every chair.

Mom told her what we did.

"You poured warm water in the toilet? Why?" the lady said. "If the snake comes up tonight, it'll get you while you're sleeping."

Augh. I never thought of that.

"Close the toilet seat. Put a heavy box on it so he can't get out," the lady said.

But she was only the first person to give us advice.

"Put food in the toilet," said Mr. Watt. "When the snake comes up to eat it, grab him."

"Set a trap for the snake," said a guy down the hall. "Like a noose. You can catch it, easy as pie."

DK's granny even had advice. "Use Drain Blaster. Pour a can of Drain Blaster down that toilet. It'll eat up that snake fast. Won't bother you no more." She blew a cloud of smoke our way. "A snake in the toilet is bad for your health."

Well, duh!

By nine-thirty all the smart visitors were gone. It was just us . . . and the snake.

We took turns going to use the Watts's bathroom. That wasn't fun. I felt really dumb walking past all of them carrying my Batman towel and toothbrush.

But that wasn't my biggest problem that day. My biggest problem had been waiting for six hours. And I didn't hear about it until Mom came into my bedroom.

"Cameron, I got a call from your principal when I was at work," she said. "Now what, exactly, did you do?"

CHAPTER 5

Kicked Out

It was late. My mom stared at me with that look. That disappointed look.

"It was just an accident," I said. "I bet the principal made it sound worse than it was."

"What's worse than swearing at a teacher and hitting him?" Mom asked.

"Let me explain . . ."

Mom stopped me. "You might think you have a good reason, Cam. But there is no excuse for attacking a teacher."

"Attack?" I said. "I just threw a dodge ball at him. The same ball he makes us throw at each other."

"Don't argue with me. You're in enough trouble already."

I swallowed hard. "How much trouble?"

Mom's eyes got all red. "You're suspended."

Kicked out of school? I couldn't believe it. "How long?"

"Three days. Then we have to talk to the principal and the teacher you hit."

"I didn't hit him."

"Then tell me what you did."

I thought about my awful day. How could I explain it all? How bad it was to see caterpillar guts on Dad's T-shirt? How bad it was to cry in front of kids who think you're a wimp anyway. How bad it was to be afraid of DK and his snake?

I was still wondering what to say when Mom sobbed. "This is all because you miss your dad. I know that, Cam. He's not here, but I am, and I'm doing my best."

We were all doing our best. But what if our best wasn't good enough?

* * *

That night I had another nightmare. The boa was after me. DK chased both of us with a can of Drain Blaster. I was glad when Mom woke me up for breakfast. I went across the hallway to the Watts's, and used their bathroom. Neither Ella nor I wanted to risk ours.

At eight o'clock Pat Piper knocked on the door. This day, he wore a brown sweater covered with dog hairs, and he carried a cage.

Pat was followed by Zoom, the super, holding a yellow poster. "Who hung this in the lobby?"

The poster said a deadly snake was loose in the building.

"We want to keep this quiet," said Zoom.

Two more people came to our door. Quiet? Fat chance.

Mom left for work, and Ella went to school.

I stayed home with a bunch of rules. No TV. No Internet. No nothing except a ton of schoolwork my mom made up for me. And a giant snake in the bathroom.

But Pat had a new idea: a rat. A white rat.

I'm not joking. Pat held a white rat, frozen in a plastic bag. A red $2.99 price tag was stuck to it.

"You can buy them at Noah's Pet Shop," Pat said. "People feed them to their pet snakes."

"A snake snack," I said. I shivered.

"Yeah, kind of. The rat is bait. When the boa comes up to get him, I'll pull the boa out and into the cage. Problem solved. Case closed."

Pat unwrapped the rat, rolled up his sleeves and sat beside the toilet. He put the rat down in the toilet with his left hand.

It sounded too easy to me, but I hung around to watch.

Then I started thinking. Yanking a big snake out of the toilet would take some force. Once it came loose, it would whip around like crazy. And what if the boa bit Pat? I'd have to pull its fangs out of Pat's bloody hand. Wait a minute – they don't have fangs. But their little teeth are as sharp as pins.

I went off to the kitchen.

An hour later, I checked on Pat. He still sat on the floor. Now his right hand held the rat in the toilet. His left hand rested red and wrinkled in his lap. "He'll come up soon," said Pat. His eyes told me he didn't believe it either.

Someone knocked at the apartment door. When I opened it, I saw a tanned lady with long blond hair. She was holding a microphone. Behind her was a guy with a camera. And behind them was a crowd of neighbors.

"We're from CITY TV," said the blond lady.

A big guy with a small camera barged in beside her. "I'm from Bay City News," he said. "Can we come in?"

Before I could answer, they were all inside our apartment.

The circus had begun.

CHAPTER 6

News From the Toilet

It was only noon, but the circus had come to my bathroom. The tanned, blond lady smiled at the camera. She spoke into a mike. "The Redwood Apartments have a new tenant. He's as long as a small car, and he keeps popping up in the toilet."

The blond lady looked pretty, and she sounded smart. Who would think she had just spit her gum into our sink?

The blond lady went on. "SPCA Officer Pat Piper says the deadly snake can live in the pipes

for weeks. In case it is hungry . . ."

The camera zoomed in on Pat. He was holding the rat in his left hand.

The blond lady finished. "The tenants here are being careful, but they are cheerful."

The camera turned to catch the crowd.

Of course, she got it wrong. No one was cheerful. Some people had poured Drain Blaster down their toilets. Some had called city hall. And all of them wanted Zoom to do something.

The camera guy shouted, "Hey, Pat. Hold the rat up higher. I need a close-up shot."

A reporter from *World News* asked a bunch of questions. "Where did this snake come from? Who owns him?"

Pat shrugged. "No one's rushing to claim it."

"Why not? A snake like that must cost a lot."

"It's not legal to keep them in the city. If we find the owner, it will mean a trip to court. And maybe a large fine."

"So who keeps dangerous snakes?" the reporter asked. "Tough guys?"

Pat shrugged. "You only hear about bad snake owners, not the good ones."

The camera man winked at me. "They make better news." Then he shook my hand. "I'm John. Would your mom mind if you went on camera?"

I didn't answer. My mom would have a fit. But she wasn't home so it was my choice.

Pat kept talking. "Most snake owners work

hard. Snakes need special food, special lights, a 'hot rock' . . ."

"How do they escape?"

"Some cages don't close tight. Some owners fall asleep when they play with the snake. Then the boa slides away, into the wallboards."

I quickly checked our walls.

"Back behind the wallboards, snakes can crawl through a whole building. When they get hungry or cold, they just pop out. "

I shuddered. That snake could be anywhere.

TV cameras kept shooting. Small cameras flashed. A make-up girl fixed the blond lady's face. Reporters shouted questions. They wrote notes, insulted each other and shared donuts. I had to admit, it was kind of exciting. I was watching the news being made. I *was* the news. Sort of.

I looked up snakes on the computer. I yelled out facts. "The longest poisonous snake is the king cobra. It will attack anything, even other cobras. Snakes' jaws are like hinges. They open wide to hold a bigger animal. Then their muscles squeeze it down into the snake's stomach."

Even Pat was looking at me. Good. If I was famous, maybe the kids at school would think I was cool.

"Sea snakes are the most poisonous . . . ," I went on, but I got cut off.

Someone screeched. "I got it! I got it!"

The whole crowd raced for our bathroom.

The *World News* reporter stood beside the toilet, grinning. "I got the boa's picture! I got it!"

No one was happy. The TV guys had missed it. The other reporters were jealous. And Pat was going nuts. He screamed at the reporter. "You made me miss it! I could have caught the boa until you screeched."

The reporter didn't care. He ran from our apartment laughing, "I got the photo and you guys didn't. You'll see it tonight in our paper."

Pat growled, "It's time to get tough."

Pencils flew. Cameras rolled. "Tell us more," they shouted.

"I'll plug an electric blanket in beside the toilet.

We'll put the rat on it."

I was glad we didn't own an electric blanket.

"So what will stop the snake from grabbing the rat and taking off?"

"Easy. I'll take the toilet off. That will leave a large hole in the floor. Then I'll put on a special valve onto the hole. The snake will stick his head through the valve. But he won't be able to back out again. He'll be stuck there until I catch him."

"Sounds smooth," said the blond TV lady.

"But there's one problem." Pat grinned like the mutt who ate the meatballs. "The snake will only come into a quiet room. So all of you get out."

"Out?" the reporters asked.

"Out. Out of the bathroom and the apartment," Pat told them. "Out!"

There was a lot of grumbling, but the reporters left. Then the apartment was quiet. Just Pat in the bathroom and me doing homework. Ella and Mom would be home soon. And I didn't have much to show for a whole day of homework.

There was a quiet knock at the door. It was Rafe.

"Were you bored staying home alone all day?" he asked.

"Alone? Are you kidding? This place was a zoo."

"Cool! What happened?"

I told him the story. Then I asked, "What are they saying about me at school?"

But before Rafe could answer, Mom came home.

She took one look around the apartment and got mad. "This place is a mess! Cameron, what have you done!?"

She was winding up for a lecture. I could feel it coming. But Rafe spoke first. "Ms. Landry sent some work home for Cameron. I can help him with it if you like."

"Oh. Thank you," said Mom. "Who are you?"

"Rafe Paz." He shook Mom's hand.

"Oh. You're the new family in 302. Thank you for helping Cam." I could see Mom's brain working. She liked this polite kid and hoped it would rub off on me.

Mom looked into the bathroom. She almost bumped into Pat on the floor.

"No progress?" she asked.

Pat grunted. He was having a hard time getting the toilet off.

Mom came back out just as the five o'clock news was starting. I pointed to the TV. The news had begun, and our bathroom was the main event.

Ella came in. All four of us stood watching our toilet on TV.

"Wow!" Mom kept saying. Then she wrinkled her nose like something smelled. "Oh no. Look at those awful old towels. Cameron, you should have hung up the new pink ones."

"Mom, there's a boa in our bathroom. No one will notice old towels," I said.

Mom shook her head. "You'd be surprised."

Mom worried about towels. But ugly towels were the least of my problems.

CHAPTER 7

They Don't Crush You

The boa went into hiding for the next two days. But that didn't stop the news. Even more reporters and camera crews crowded our apartment. They shouted questions in French, Spanish and Japanese. Our boa had become world news.

But we were tired of it. Our floors were dirty. A TV camera had bashed a dent in the hall wall. Friday Mom looked in the fridge for some fried chicken. It was gone. We never found out who ate it.

On Saturday, Ella and I watched the action around us.

"We could make money selling them drinks," I said.

Ella scowled. "They'd spill it on the rug. Look at this place. It's like the park after a rock concert. I hate this. And I'm sick of not being able to use my own bathroom."

"Cheer up," I grinned. "It could be worse."

"How?"

"You could have the flu."

Ella grabbed her purse and headed for the door. "I'm off to the mall."

Mom handed her a sweater and too much advice.

"Can I go out too?" I asked.

"No. You're suspended from school."

"But it's Saturday."

"We talk to your principal on Monday. Then you can go out. Maybe. In the meantime, you're grounded."

"But I need exercise."

"Walk downstairs and get the laundry from the dryer."

"Awh, you look so pretty today, Mom."

"Downstairs, kid."

I came out of the laundry room lugging a basket of clothes. DK stood in the hall. He smelled like an ashtray. "Still got a snake in the can?"

Stay cool, I told myself. *Don't back away*. "Still smoking in the back room, DK?"

"Want me to punch you?"

"Want me to tell your granny about your secret smoking spot?" I pushed the elevator button.

"Everybody at school is laughing at you, Crybaby."

That hurt more than a punch.

I rushed into the elevator, but DK tripped me. I landed on the floor with shirts and underwear hanging all over me. DK laughed. But this time I didn't start crying.

I went into our apartment. The news people had gone. Mom was leaving. "I can't stay to watch this."

"Watch what?" I asked.

"Pat has a guinea pig in the bathroom. It's fluffy and it's shaking."

"Why?"

"He's using it as bait."

"The rat didn't work."

"The rat was dead, the guinea pig is alive," Mom said. "Pat has him in a cage. The bars are just far enough apart to let the snake slide in. After the snake eats the guinea pig, it will be too fat to get out."

"You're kidding."

Mom didn't even smile.

I felt sick. I cut up an apple for the guinea pig. Then I crossed the hall to the Watts's bathroom. It was still steamy. I shut the toilet seat lid and sat down. Mr. Watt's blue bath towel hung over the shower rod. His razor lay by the sink. How I missed those things in our bathroom. My dad had his shaving cream and his special stuff. And I missed that, just like I missed him.

I leaned back and closed my eyes. I let the

48

peace and the smells of someone else's dad comfort me. Then Mrs. Watt coughed outside the door. It was time to go.

Rafe stood at my door. "Wanna play my new video game?"

"I'm grounded," I said.

"Well, we're still in the same building," he replied. And that was true. It was the same *ground*, really.

I was glad not to go home yet. We played Jungle King on his Xbox. We zapped lions and killed headhunters with spears. Then a huge snake dropped from a tree and killed me.

"I can't get away from those slimy snakes!" I yelled.

"They're not slimy," said Rafe.

"How do you know?"

"I touched one."

"Gross. Where?" I asked.

"At the zoo back in Texas."

"You touched a snake!" I shivered. "What was it like?"

"Dry, cool. Smooth, like a leather belt."

I looked at Rafe with new respect. "Were you scared it might bite?"

"Not much. If you hold a snake by the neck, there's not much it can do. The zookeepers said there's more chance of getting bitten by a dog. Snakes are scared of us too."

I shuddered. "Still, I don't want to be crushed by a boa."

Rafe laughed. "They don't really crush you. They squeeze tighter and tighter until there's no room left for you to breathe."

My neck felt tight. I coughed. Rafe showed me a YouTube video about boas. I think he wanted me to feel better, but it didn't help.

CHAPTER 8

Locked In

R afe and I stood outside my bathroom. He was the one who opened the door. I peeked inside, ready to throw up.

But there was no reason to. The guinea pig sat munching my apple. And there was no boa in sight.

I had just closed the door when Zoom came in with a long pole. A steel rope hung from it. "I think this plumber's snake will do the trick," he said. "If it works for clogged toilets, it'll work for your snake."

"No you don't!" yelled Rafe. He grabbed the plumber's snake. "See this hook on the end of it."

Zoom grinned. "Yup. That'll get your snake good."

Rafe frowned. "It will cut the poor snake and kill it."

"So?" said Zoom. "It's a snake."

"It's a living creature." Rafe stood right in front of Zoom.

"It shouldn't be in our toilets."

"You can't punish the snake for its sloppy owner."

Much as I hated that snake in my toilet, I had to agree with Rafe. I stood beside him with my arms folded. "No way you're going to hurt that snake."

"My friend is right," said Rafe.

Zoom sighed and twisted off the hook. "Okay, but I need to check." Then he pushed the plumber's snake down the toilet drain. We watched and waited. Zoom reached the end of his snake, about twice as long as he was tall.

Nothing. The boa was no longer in our toilet pipe.

But where had it gone?

When Ella came home, we went up to 302 for dinner. It was like we'd died and gone to heaven. Mrs. Paz served tea. Mum plopped into a chair. Ella talked to Jade about girl stuff. I followed Rafe to his room to play video games. "Anything that doesn't have snakes in it," I said. But our minds were on snakes anyway.

Then we had some kind of Mexican meal. The chili tasted great, and there was some wrapped stuff, too. Rafe's dad told jokes. We laughed a lot. Too soon it was time to go.

"That felt like a week's holiday," said Mom as we walked down the stairs.

She was right. Between bathroom problems and snake problems and school problems, we were all beat.

DK's granny met us in the hall. She didn't have a smoke, for once. Her face was wrinkled with worry. "Have you seen DK?"

We shook our heads.

"I can't find the kid anywhere."

That's good news, I thought.

DK's granny sobbed, "I phoned all over. I looked everywhere. Maybe that awful snake ate my little guy."

Unlikely, I thought, but I could always hope.

"If we see him, we'll be sure to let you know," Mom promised.

Something bugged me but I kept quiet. DK was no friend of mine.

We got back to our apartment. Pat had put our toilet back in place. But Ella still wouldn't use it.

I tried to watch TV, but I couldn't. I knew where DK probably was. Of course, he'd beat me up if I told, but maybe he was in trouble. Maybe his granny was right.

I slipped out to tell the old lady where DK might be. But then I thought again. DK would kill me if I blabbed. So maybe I should go and find him myself.

I took the elevator all the way down. The basement hall was creepy at night. I didn't like the long, thin shadows. Or the strange hissing noises.

I could see that the door to the back room was wedged open. I pulled the door open wider and peeked in. At first the room looked empty. Then I saw DK.

He was flattened against the far wall of the

room. His eyes were wide open. Weird.

So I stepped inside. Then I saw why DK was so scared.

The boa was coiled up by the drain hole in the floor. It looked huge. And it waited between DK and the door.

The door! The door that had just swung shut behind me.

I jiggled the rusty handle. I pushed the door with my hand. Then with two hands. Then with my shoulder. But the door was stuck shut or locked tight.

I was locked inside with a bully and a giant boa.

CHAPTER 9

In the Dark

"Why did you go and shut the door?" DK whispered.

"I didn't mean to. I came down here because your granny's upset."

"If you told her about my secret room, I'll punch..."

I knew he couldn't punch me. The snake blocked him.

The snake's tail moved. It oozed forward in curves. Soon its head was getting close to DK.

DK gasped.

Now I don't like DK, but I didn't want to watch a snake kill him. And once the boa got him, then I was next. So I tried to come up with a plan.

Should I throw something at it? What good would that do? DK was too scared to move, and if he did, that would be the worst thing. Going fast is the wrong way to get away from a snake. Snakes don't see or hear well. They find prey by sensing heat. Running makes us get even hotter.

The snake turned its head. Its tongue flicked in and out.

Checking for dinner? I thought. There was a dead mouse in the corner, but we probably looked tastier.

I shivered. It was cold down here.

Cold! That was it. The boa was looking for heat. It wanted the hot water pipes above DK's head. Not food. Not DK.

"Hey, DK," I said. "I've got a hunch about that

snake. I don't think he wants you. Even snakes
have taste. Just back away slowly, before he gets
closer."

DK shook. He was too scared to move.

The snake slid closer. DK mewed like a crying
kitten. Somebody had to do something.

I guess it had to be me.

I took a deep breath. Slowly I edged around

the room. My heart beat so loudly it echoed in my head. I didn't look at the snake.

At last I reached DK. Now the snake had a choice of two meals. But my hunch was that he didn't want to eat either of us.

"We're dead. We're both dead," DK whined. Tears rolled down his cheek.

What a suck, I thought. I grabbed DK's hand and pulled him along the wall. Slow. Dead slow. It seemed like hours before we got back to the door.

DK gasped and pointed at the snake. The boa was moving.

But not toward us. The snake glided up to the hot water pipes and curled around them. We were safe. For now.

"Didn't I tell you?" I whispered.

"Yeah, but how do we get out of here?" DK whined. "You let the door close."

DK pushed on the door. He hit the handle. It wouldn't open.

"Can we call for help?" I asked.

"Nobody comes down here," DK whispered

back. "No one in the laundry room will hear us over the noise of the machines." He kicked the door. "We'll die before someone finds us." DK's body shook. His nose ran.

I had to stay cool. I looked around for one more idea. Then I got it.

"Where are you going?" DK asked.

"I want to try something," I said, moving along the wall toward the electrical panel.

"Just don't leave me alone," begged DK. He followed me like a scared puppy.

The electrical panel was old, like the rest of our building. It had four rows of circuit breakers. The labels were too faded to read, but I knew how they worked.

I pointed to the panel. "That's how we'll bring someone down here."

"Why would anyone check it at night?" asked DK.

"They'd have to. If the lights went off," I said.

"What do you mean?"

"That panel controls all the power in the

building. If I can somehow figure out which of these breakers to flip, I can turn off the lights."

DK stared at me. "The … lights … off? In here too?"

I hadn't thought of that. "Got a better idea?" I said.

"No way. I'm not staying in the dark with that snake."

I nodded. We stood by the panel and waited. For what?

"Look!" DK grabbed my arm.

The snake was moving again. Maybe the pipes were too hot. Maybe it was getting hungry. Either way, it slid along a pipe toward us.

DK burst into tears. Now which one of us was the crybaby?

The snake lifted its head like it was hunting.

"Quiet, DK," I said. "It thinks you're dinner." I was amazed how strong I sounded.

I checked the breakers again. Which ones lit the first floor?

I took a deep breath. I skipped the first two

breakers. They had to be the basement. I flipped the third breaker.

Relief. Our light stayed on. But I had to make sure the lights would go off upstairs.

I flipped another breaker. There was a spark, then nothing more. The boa was coming closer still.

I froze. DK crumpled to the floor. The boa didn't care.

I listened but heard nothing outside. No more time to waste. I flipped four more breakers.

My luck died. The room went as black as a garbage bag.

CHAPTER 10

Holding Tight

In the dark, I hugged the wall. Then something grabbed my leg. It was DK. He pulled himself up and sobbed.

But then a miracle happened. An emergency light came on. We could see.

DK grinned at me. "Maybe you're smarter than I thought."

Why should I change his mind?

Then I froze. The boa was creeping toward us again.

"I hear footsteps!" whispered DK. "Outside."

The snake slid under the beam of light. Its eyes glowed green. Its body shone like brown glass. It kept coming toward us.

I pulled DK back toward the door, but the snake was coming toward the door too. There were voices outside, in the hall. But the door was locked. And even if they got it open, the snake would attack.

Somehow I had to keep the snake away from the door. But how? Could I hold it back? Rafe had held a snake and he didn't get killed. Maybe I'd be safe if I did it right.

If I did it right.

I looked at DK. He's bigger, but he was shaking and crying.

It had to be me.

There was shouting outside. The door handle moved.

It had to be now.

I stepped close to

the snake. I held my breath. I said a little prayer. Then I reached out with my right hand and grabbed its neck.

"We're in here!" I shouted. There was no reason to be quiet now.

The boa squirmed, but I held on tight. With my left hand, I grabbed the boa down near its tail. That's how they did it on the YouTube video. Now its tail could wrap around my arm, but not my body.

Outside, someone grunted and pushed the door. I stepped back. If the door slammed into me, I'd lose my grip on the snake.

We heard keys, and then the door opened. A bright light shone at us.

The boa jerked so hard my left arm flew up with it.

DK squealed.

And Zoom didn't know what to say. He stood there with old Mr. Kim and just stared.

"We could use a little help," I grunted. The snake was way stronger than I was. And now he was scared.

Mr. Kim got the message. "Zoom, you run upstairs and bring down the cage. Fast. I'll stay with the boys."

As soon as Zoom went out the door, DK raced after him. *Thanks for all the help*, I thought.

I didn't know how long I could hold that boa. Its tail was wrapped tightly around my arm. It kept jerking to get free.

I looked at old Mr. Kim. "Maybe you can get hold of the tail," I said.

"Moving too fast for me, boy," he replied. "But I'll do something if he starts curling around you."

Yeah, great, I thought. Nothing like an eighty-year-old guy to pull a boa off me.

But Zoom came back pretty quickly. My mom and Ella ran behind him. Mom looked sickly pale. Ella just shook her head, amazed.

Zoom set the cage on the floor in front of me. He opened the door wide.

"So what now?" I asked. I had a snake wrapped around my arm. And I was losing it.

"I'll call the cops," Zoom said.

"We haven't got time!" I yelled. "This snake wants to eat."

That's when my sister – my scared-of-snakes sister – moved. She bent down on the floor, looked the other way and picked up the dead mouse. And threw it in the cage.

Perfect, I thought. I brought the boa over to the cage door, head first.

"Time for dinner," I said. Then I pulled my hands back real fast. And the snake slithered into the cage.

Zoom slammed the door of the cage shut.

Mom rushed to hug me. She laughed and cried. I'm not sure what I did, but I was pretty happy. And my sister, she was in shock. "I touched a mouse. I touched a dead mouse. With my bare hands."

* * *

So now I'm a hero. The news people came once more – for me. My picture and story were big news. I pulled Ella into the pictures too. She picked up a dead mouse – to save me.

The snake? It's in the hospital. It got hurt from too much Drain Blaster.

And I'm back in school. Mr. Hogan understood about the dodge ball. It was an accident, that's all.

DK is nice to me now. Not because I saved him, but because I didn't tell anyone that he cried like a baby that night.

I have only one problem left. My sister.

Ella says, "I touched a dead mouse for you, Cam. You owe me big time."

G.T. SHERMAN is the author of *Grave Danger*, published in four languages, and other award-winning novels. She has been an elementary school teacher and a school librarian, and has taught creative writing at the college level for almost twenty years. Recently, she's been taking small parts as an actor in various films and television shows.

For more information on HIP novels:

 High Interest Publishing – Publishers of H·I·P Books
www.hip-books.com